A Corisi Christmas

Book 7: A novella

The Legacy Collection

Ruth Cardello

Author Contact

website: RuthCardello.com

email: Minouri@aol.com

Facebook: Author Ruth Cardello

Twitter: RuthieCardello

Warm up with the couple who started it all. Dominic and Abby are celebrating Christmas—Corisi style. This holiday NOVELLA is a heartwarming visit with the Legacy gang. You'll laugh. You'll cry. You'll want to read the series all over again.

The Legacy Collection:

Also available in audiobook format

Where my billionaires began.

Book 1: Maid for the Billionaire (available at all major eBook stores for FREE!)

Book 2: For Love or Legacy

Book 3: Bedding the Billionaire

Book 4: Saving the Sheikh

Book 5: Rise of the Billionaire

Book 6: Breaching the Billionaire: Alethea's Redemption

Book 7: A Corisi Christmas Novella

Be the first to hear about my releases

One random newsletter subscriber will be chosen every month in 2015. The chosen subscriber will receive a $100 eGift Card! Sign up today at ruthcardello.com!

Copyright

A Corisi Christmas

Print Edition

Dedication

This book is dedicated to my in-laws, the Cardellos. They've welcomed me as warmly as the Andrades welcomed Nicole. I'll happily be spending Christmas Day with them again this year and grateful to have them in my life.

A Note to My Readers

As the youngest of eleven children, I wasn't raised in a family that ever had much money. My parents made Christmas magical anyway. Each Christmas Eve all the children would gather in the living room of my parents' home to wait for the sound of bells that announced Santa's sleigh landing on the roof. We always heard the heavy sound of Santa's boots as he walked down the stairs of our home. Santa had one gift for each child. Just one. Usually it was what we asked for, but sometimes it wasn't. If we had our hearts set on a gift Santa couldn't afford for Christmas, sometimes it would arrive later in the year—if we were very good.

We learned to be realistic about our requests and grateful for what we received. We were also told each year that the greatest gift was having the family gathered and to remember the real reason for the holiday was a celebration of our beliefs.

With my own children, it's hard to not want to give them everything. When I read over the long list of what they ask for, I remind myself that the importance of the holiday is found in the love we show each other and the traditions we pass on. My parents are no longer with us, but the magic they created is still very much alive.

Even though we have to rent a house big enough to accommodate how large my family has become, Santa still rings his bells when he lands on the roof. He still stomps down the stairs with one present for each child. Three generations gather and that is the most important present I give my children each year. I remind them to be grateful for our family and thankful to God. I hope that's what they pass on to their children.

Whatever holiday you celebrate, my wish for you is that yours is full of love and hope this season.

Chapter One

"YOU'RE SURE WE weren't followed?" Nicole Andrade asked her driver when the car came to a stop. Her hands shook as she buttoned her long coat.

"I was careful to be discrete, Mrs. Andrade."

Arnold had been Nicole's driver for as long as she could remember, since her early childhood. He'd stayed with her out of loyalty rather than necessity. To Nicole, he was more family than employee, and she had told him that several times. There was no need for formality between them, but Arnold was old-fashioned and Nicole respected that about him.

"I feel like a traitor when I come here."

Arnold met her eyes in the rearview mirror. The sympathy in his expression was a comfort. Not many would understand how Nicole could have everything and still wake up scared in the middle of the night. She was happily married; she not only had her brother back in her life, but she also had a large extended family who loved her.

And yet I keep coming back.

"Would you like me to get the flowers from the back,

Mrs. Andrade?"

"I need a moment, Arnold." Arnold left the car running and waited without a word. Nicole slowly covered her cold hands with her leather gloves. "I should be glad he's gone."

"He was your father," Arnold said gently.

Nicole blinked back a tear. "A father who drove my mother into hiding, beat my brother until he left, and then ignored the only one who stayed with him—me. How could I still love him?"

Arnold didn't answer, but Nicole didn't expect him to. As always, he was quietly supportive yet held his opinions to himself. If danger came, Nicole didn't doubt that Arnold would defend her even at the risk of his own life, but he wouldn't discuss it afterward. That he listened while she rambled on about her life was a testament to his affection for her. He was a private man.

His silence made him one of the few Nicole felt comfortable opening up to. "Stephan finished our house on Isola Santos. He gave Gio the original Andrade house. We could have lived in the home my brother built on the other side of the island, but Stephan wanted something more traditional. Our new house is beautiful. Tasteful. Perfect. When Stephan first told me we could demolish Dominic's complex, I was okay with it, but now that it's scheduled, I don't want to see them remove it. I want to throw myself in front of it and beg for someone to save it. Even Dominic said he was fine with it being torn down. I should let it go."

Arnold opened his mouth as if he was about to say something, then closed it, and met her eyes in the mirror again.

"I know it's just a house, Arnold. Just a glass and chrome monstrosity. An eyesore to most people. But that island, for however much trouble it has caused, brought us all together. It was a place for both Andrades and Corisis. That's about to change, and I don't know if I'm ready." Nicole put a hand on her stomach. "I'm pregnant, Arnold. This should be the happiest time of my life. I thank God every day that so many people care about me now, but I'm falling apart on the inside."

Arnold turned in his seat and put his hand out to Nicole. She held on to his tightly.

"Stephan and I weren't trying to have a baby. I haven't told anyone about the baby yet because I don't know how I feel. I want children. So, part of me is happy, but another part is terrified. What if I can't be a better mother than mine was?" Nicole looked out the window of the car in the direction of her father's headstone. "And why do I come here for answers from a man who gave me none while he was alive?"

"Nicole," Arnold said her name in the way a father does with a child, "you're too hard on yourself. You will be a wonderful mother."

Nicole wiped away a tear that had escaped down her cheek. "That's kind of you to say, Arnold, but is it true? Stephan's family has welcomed me as one of their own. They are warm, loving, and better to me than my own family ever was. Why isn't that enough? Thanksgiving was perfect. I should have loved it, but all I could think about was what I had to leave behind to belong there. I feel like I'm losing myself. How can I raise a child when I'm not sure who I am anymore?"

Arnold cleared his throat. "You need to talk to your husband, Nicole. Let him be there for you." With that, he released Nicole's hand and turned back toward the steering wheel, a move that was Arnold's way of bringing the invisible wall back up between them. Someone else might have taken the action as a sign that he didn't care, but Nicole knew better.

"Thank you, Arnold. Now, please retrieve the flowers from the trunk and help me carry them to my father's grave."

"Yes, Mrs. Andrade," Arnold said and opened his door before coming around to open hers.

"DADDY!"

Without taking the time to remove his coat, Dominic Corisi dropped to one knee and braced himself as his young daughter threw herself into his arms. He stood, picking her up as he did. "Hey, Princess." He walked with Judy over to give his wife a quick kiss. Abby kissed him in greeting but didn't look happy. "I know I said I'd be home earlier. Sorry, Victor and Alessandro came to see me at the office. You know how those two can talk."

Abby gave Judy a pointed look. "Judy, do you have something to tell your father?"

Dominic laughed. "Uh oh. That's Mommy's teacher voice. What did you do, Judy?"

"Dominic," Abby said in reprimand, "this is serious."

Dominic forced a frown on his face, but he knew Judy saw right through it. "Let me guess, you hid the housekeeper's keys again."

Judy shook her head. "Worse."

"You let the dog out into the garden."

Judy covered her mouth and giggled. "Mr. Kirsten was so mad that day. Nope. I know not to do that anymore."

"Tell him, Judy."

Judy tilted her head to one side and gave Dominic sad little eyes that nearly broke his heart. "Maybe my teacher gave me a bad note."

"That's it, she's fired," Dominic said but wisely stopped smiling when he saw Abby's eyes narrow.

Judy's eyes rounded in horror and her bottom lip quivered. "I love Mrs. Liseika. Don't fire her."

Abby rushed over to reassure Judy, and gave Dominic a light swat. "Dom, she's too young to joke with like that. Judy, your father would never have Mrs. Liseika fired."

"Unless she needed to be let go," Dominic said seriously.

Abby sighed and sent Dominic a painfully clear message with her eyes. It wasn't that Dominic didn't believe all children needed discipline, but Judy was only five. Dominic had been raised in a house full of fear and violence. He refused to expose his family to either. Abby said he was too soft on Judy. He didn't disagree with his wife, but he wasn't about to change either. If Abby gave Judy a consequence, he supported that decision, but he kept all anger out of his house.

Dominic put Judy down. "Show me the note."

Judy retrieved the note from a folder on the counter and handed it to Dominic. "I don't think I should be in trouble. I was like a superhero."

Dominic scanned the note then looked across at Abby. "What kind of private school is this? They let the kids brawl on the playground? I told you we should have our security in the building."

Abby shook her head. "You are not sending Marc Stone or any of his goons into an elementary school. We want Judy to have a normal childhood. It's a good school, Dominic, the best in the city. There wasn't actually a fight until your daughter threw a punch."

Dominic looked down at Judy. "You know you're not supposed to hit anyone."

Judy lowered her eyes then gave another adorably soulful look up at him. "Dad, you would have punched him, too. There is a new boy, Lucas, in our class who gets stuck on words when he talks. He talks this this: Nice to m-m-m-meet y-y-you."

"It's called stuttering. The boy stutters," Abby said.

"Okay, so he was trying to say something and this big kid came over and started laughing at him. Lucas told him to st-st-st-op. And the big kid kept laughing at him. I told him to stop, but he wouldn't, and Lucas started to cry. The big kid called him a sissy and pushed him, so I punched him."

Dominic met his wife's eyes over Judy's head. "Sounds like she did the right thing."

Abby rubbed a hand over her eyes. "If we didn't live in a society with rules, maybe. Judy, what could you have done instead of punching the boy who was laughing at your friend?"

Judy made a face. "I could have told the teacher."

"And what would the teacher have done?"

"She would have told the boy to stop."

"So you didn't have to hit anyone, did you?"

Judy gave her father an imploring look. "Dad, sometimes mean kids get sneaky mean when you tell. Or they call you a tattletale. I'm not a tattletale. Lucas is my friend, and if that boy makes Lucas cry tomorrow, I'll punch him again."

Abby crouched before her daughter so they were eye to eye. "You are not punching anyone, understood? I'll speak to the teacher tonight, and we'll make sure no one bothers your friend tomorrow. Deal? Let us take care of this. You just keep your hands to yourself."

Dominic nodded in agreement. "Judy, what's the older boy's name? Do you know it?"

Before Judy could answer, Abby straightened and said, "Judy, Mrs. Kirsten is tidying the living room. Could you ask her if you could help her?"

"I thought we were going to the library tonight."

"That was before you got a bad note from school. Go find Mrs. Kirsten, please."

"Dad?" Judy looked to Dominic sadly.

"You heard your mother. Go."

Once Judy was out of the kitchen Abby walked over to Dominic, shaking her head. He slid his arms around her and pulled her to him for a kiss. He felt the tension ebb out of her as the kiss deepened.

She broke off the kiss first, but she was smiling. She wagged a finger at him. "Don't try to distract me. This is serious stuff."

Dominic nuzzled the spot on Abby's neck he knew drove her wild. Her breath became shallow, and her hand tightened on his shoulder. He loved how quickly the heat still flared between them nearly six years and one child later. "It is. I'm listening."

Abby's lids lowered and her eyes burned with desire as he continued his gentle assault. "We don't want Judy to think violence is the answer."

Dominic's mouth stilled. "Sometimes it is, Abby. No one threatens my family or my friends. I protect what is mine, and Judy takes after me in that respect."

Abby laid a hand on Dominic's cheek. "Dom, you and Judy may have some of the same qualities, but she's not growing up in the household you did. Your father—"

Dominic pulled away from Abby. "Can we not make this about my father? He's dead, along with any desire I ever had to talk about him."

Abby stepped in front of Dominic. "Look at me, Dom. Don't pull away. I love you just the way you are. We both want the same thing for Judy. We want her to grow up happy, healthy, and strong. I'm merely suggesting she can be strong without getting physical. If you don't want to see her thrown out of every private school in New York, we need to nip this in the bud. I know she's your little princess, but she's going to be our little devil if we don't set boundaries."

Dominic sighed, wrapped his arms around Abby again,

and rested his chin on top of her head. She was right. "I'll talk to her. I do want the name of the boy who was bothering her friend, though."

Abby hugged her husband tightly, and he felt her chuckle. "No, you don't. You are not calling his father and threatening him."

"He should know what his son is doing."

"I'll make sure the school contacts his father."

Dominic looked into Abby's eyes and marveled at the emotion he saw there. She might not agree with him, but she loved him, and he was a better man because of it. He couldn't imagine his life without her. The mere thought of it rekindled his desire for her. "How long do you think we have before Mrs. Kirsten sends Judy back in here?"

Abby laughed and snuggled against him. "I could text her and ask her to take Judy for a walk. That would buy us at least half an hour."

Dominic swung Abby up into his arms and started up the stairway that led to their bedroom. "Ask her if she can delay dinner tonight. What I have in mind shouldn't be rushed."

Chapter Two

THE NEXT DAY Nicole stopped by her brother's home. He wouldn't be there yet, but his wife would. She and Abby had become close over the past five or so years. Outside of Arnold, Abby was the one Nicole turned to when she needed to talk something out. Unlike some members of the family, she could keep a secret.

One of their staff led Nicole to where Abby was working in her home office. As soon as Abby saw her she closed out of the document she was typing in and stood. "Nicole, I didn't know you were coming by today."

"I was hoping to catch you while you weren't busy."

Abby hugged Nicole in greeting. "I'm always busy, but that's what happens when you try to cram everything into the hours when your child is at school. Hey, have a seat. Are you hungry?"

Nicole shook her head and sat down. Her stomach was queasy more mornings than not lately, and she didn't want to test it. "What are you working on?"

Abby waved a hand at the computer and took a seat across from Nicole. "We're trying to get more schools into

Boltatia, but the government isn't making it easy. We have the funds, but every time I think we've jumped through all the right hoops, they add more. It'll work out, though. It always does. How are you?"

Nicole crossed one leg over the other and clasped her hands on her lap. "I'm a mess."

Abby scooted closer. "Oh, no. What's wrong?"

"Nothing and everything."

"Did something happen with Stephan?"

Nicole shook her head. "No."

Abby looked at her with a sympathetic expression. "You have to give me something to go on here."

Nicole took a deep breath then asked, "Do you ever not want to go over to the Andrades' for the holidays?"

Abby laid a hand on Nicole's in support. "Sometimes. They're wonderful, but their gatherings can be overwhelming. Thanksgiving was over one hundred people. It's not exactly the way I grew up."

"Dominic loves it there, doesn't he?"

Abby gave Nicole a long look before answering. "He loves *them*. I don't know if he loves the chaos that always ensues at their parties, but we're grateful they've welcomed us into their family. It means we can spend more time with you and Stephan, too."

"Do you ever miss spending time with just your sister and her family?"

"I do that, too. Lil and I have our own holiday, but we do it a week before. We consider it our warm-up to the festivities, and it gives us time to reminisce, keep some of our family traditions going. Things like that."

"I didn't realize you did that," Nicole said, feeling some of her guilt fall away.

"We don't make a big deal out of it. We don't want anyone to feel excluded, but it's our time when we remember our parents and our own childhood. Is that something you want to do with Dominic? You should have said something. We can get together."

"I'd like that." Abby was an angel, and a perceptive one at that. "Lately I've been thinking about my family and our Christmas traditions. Does Dominic ever talk about them?"

"No," Abby said with a sad shake of her head.

Nicole took a deep breath and shared a story she'd kept to herself over the years. "Our father didn't believe in the holiday, and our mother was too afraid to push the issue. He considered presents and decoration clutter. We had a formal holiday dinner; that was all he allowed. When Dominic and I were little we used to have secret celebrations. We were too young to have money of our own, so we would steal things out of each other's rooms and wrap them up in paper we'd beg off the staff. We didn't care that we were giving each other things we already had; it was our special tradition."

"That's so sad, but beautiful in a way." Abby sniffed and wiped a corner of her eye. "Dominic doesn't like to look back at that time."

"I know. I tried to bring it up once, but he got angry."

Abby put a hand on Nicole's. "Not at you, Nicole."

"That's what I told myself, but it hurt. Dominic and I used to be so close. We could talk about anything. But now I feel like our relationship depends on me pretending our whole childhood never happened. But it did, Abby, and I don't want to be ashamed of who I am anymore."

"Ashamed? Nicole, you have nothing to be ashamed of."

"I wish I were as certain. Our mother left us, and I've always considered her weak for it, but I stayed because I was too scared to leave."

"Oh, Nicole. You and Dominic had an abusive father. Nothing that happened to you was your fault. All any of that says about you is that you were a normal child who should never have been faced with the choices you were given."

Nicole brought a shaking hand up to her mouth. "I'm pregnant, Abby, and I'm terrified. Our mother let us believe she was dead for years because she was too afraid to stand up to our father. I want to think I'm better than that, but I don't know if I am. When I think of a mother, a good one, I think of someone like you. You're strong. You don't let anything scare you. I'm not like that. I worry about things and then overthink them and hate that I can't stop myself from going in these circles in my head. I know I should be happy. I have a wonderful husband and so many people who care about me, but I'm still too scared to stand up and say what I want. What kind of mother is that?"

Abby gave Nicole's hand a little shake. "Stop. What do you want that you're so afraid of asking for?"

Nicole had asked herself the same question many times recently and was only beginning to figure it out. "I miss Dominic. I don't want to only see him when we're in a crowd of other people. I want my big brother back. Christmas is a time for new beginnings. I know my baby will have many wonderful holidays with the Andrades. My child will never be lonely or want for anything. I know that. But, this year, before everything changes, I'd like to have a small Christmas: you, Dominic, Judy, Stephan, and me. For just one year, I don't want to go to the Andrades' Christmas. There. I said it."

"Have you said anything to Stephan about this?"

"No."

"Oh, sweetie. I'm sure he'd understand. Does he know you're pregnant?"

"Not yet."

"Are you afraid he won't be happy? That man loves you. He's going to be over-the-moon happy when he finds out."

"Every time I think about telling Stephan, I get all confused. How do I tell him that the baby makes me want more? His family has been nothing but amazing to me. What if he thinks I'm ungrateful? What if . . ."

Abby put an arm around Nicole's shoulder. "Nicole, your feelings are normal. You and Dominic are survivors. What you saw, how you were raised, it doesn't go away. You both dealt with it in different ways, but that doesn't make one more right than the other. Dominic chose to fight, and he still struggles with seeing everything as a fight. You feel you were left behind, and that's why you worry that people will leave." Abby's eyes teared up. "I'm a perfectionist because I was left in charge, and I thought I had to be perfect or everything would fall apart. Trust me, we're all screwed up in our own way, but that doesn't mean we don't want better for our children. You want to work through your issues with your brother before you bring your child into the world. I'd say that's not only natural, but it's a sign that you'll make an amazing mother."

Nicole's sight blurred with tears. "You really think so?"

"I really do."

"I always feel better when I talk to you."

Abby cleared her throat. "After years of hearing the opposite from my sister while I was raising her, those are welcome words. Now, let's see if we can unravel this *mess* you think you're in. First, congratulations, Nicole, you're going to have a baby."

Nicole hugged Abby, who warmly hugged her back. "I'm going to have a baby."

"Second, come to dinner tomorrow night, and we'll see if we can't get you the Christmas you're yearning for." Abby straightened and met Nicole's eyes. "And third, holy shit, Nicole, you need to tell Stephan you're pregnant."

STEPHAN ANDRADE PUSHED back from his office desk and took out his cell phone. He was late to what would be a packed afternoon of meetings. There was a time when they would have been his first priority, but he was a different man, and until just recently, he would have said a happier one.

He thought back to the day his wife had walked into this very office and asked him to help her block her brother from taking over her family's company. His heart had been dark back then, and all he had seen was the opportunity to take down a man he'd thought had once hurt his family.

How times had changed. He wouldn't say that he and Dominic were the best of friends, but they were on the same team now. Their love of Nicole was a bond that made all else irrelevant.

Nicole was, and would always be, the best thing that ever happened to him. She'd brought joy back into his life and smoothed over the rift between him and his family. She was his lover, his best friend, and one day the mother of his children. He'd thought her beautiful the day she'd walked back into his life, but years together and his love for her had deepened his attraction to her.

In his family, she was a swan in a gaggle of wild geese. Standing out was something he knew she worried about, but he loved her more for that. Her beauty, inside and out, was a delicate one. No matter how many times he woke up beside her, or came home to her, the wonder that she was his didn't lessen.

Although he considered himself lucky to be part of a large extended family, raised by parents who loved him, being an Andrade was a blessing and a curse at times. He didn't say it, but there were times he yearned for the peace he'd found when he'd lived in California.

Family, even one as wonderful as his, could be draining in large doses. He wondered if that was why Nicole seemed withdrawn. Normally she said she loved to be with his family, but he'd noticed at Thanksgiving she hadn't been happy. The signs were subtle and no one had mentioned it, but he was certain something was bothering her.

She'd denied she was upset when he'd asked her. Still, a husband knows his wife. He knows when she's not happy, when she's pretending to sleep instead of welcoming him into her arms at night, and when she's lying.

What he didn't know was why.

Stephan looked out the window at the New York skyline. Nicole's childhood hadn't been an easy one. He knew she struggled with anxiety at times, especially around the holidays. It wasn't something she was comfortable discussing with him and that was the only area of his marriage that concerned him. He had hoped time would prove to her that his love was unwavering.

Instead, she kept her fears to herself and lied. They were small lies. She'd told him she was going shopping, but he'd found out she'd visited the doctor. She said she was visiting a friend, but she'd gone to her father's grave. Ever since their family had been threatened by the man who had almost taken Stephan's life, he'd paid a security team to watch over Nicole. Unlike Dominic, his security knew to blend into the background, so discrete it was easy to forget they were there. Apparently, Nicole had.

He could have confronted her, but he understood Nicole needed time to work things out before she brought them to him. He'd grown up in a house where issues were resolved much more quickly. People got angry, yelled things out, then made up. It had taken Stephan time to understand that in Nicole's experience, questions were traps, and tempers were something to be feared. For her, he'd learned to keep his tone low and his patience high. Waiting for Nicole to come to him with a concern had at times driven him nearly insane, but it was worth it when she finally opened up and let him in.

He thought of the time he had suggested his company absorb her father's. Financially it had made sense, and she had moved on from wanting to run it to working with charities with his mother. She'd agreed to the plan, but as they met with lawyers to formalize the move, she'd grown more and more withdrawn. Eventually she'd come to him and said she couldn't bear to close the doors on her father's company, even if the employees were brought into Stephan's. Reversing the decision had proven tricky, but he'd done it for her.

He'd do anything to make her happy. She was his wife, the reason he woke up smiling each day. Nothing was more important to him.

He felt a little guilty when he called the head of his security team and asked where she'd been. She'd gone to see her brother's wife. Even though there was nothing out of the ordinary about that, Stephan's stomach twisted at the news.

Something was wrong. He could feel it. Was she sick and afraid to tell him? She was a part of him, and he would be by her side no matter what challenges came their way.

He told his secretary to clear his afternoon and reschedule his meetings. He called Nicole as he drove back to their house, but she didn't answer, and a hundred possibilities flew through his head. None of them good.

He rushed into the house and came to a stop just before entering the family room. Nicole was sitting at her small desk in front of their large bay window. From where he stood he could see his wife's profile and the worry she hid from him was clearly displayed in her expression. Her laptop was open, but the screen had gone dark, and she was staring out the window lost in her thoughts.

She looked up as he entered the room, stood, and smiled. "Stephan, you're home early."

He walked over to her and studied her face. Had he not seen her a moment before she'd heard him, he would have thought she was in a good mood. "I called, but you didn't answer."

"My phone must still be in my purse." She scanned the room then gave him an apologetic look. "I bet I left it in the kitchen. Sorry."

He pulled her gently into his arms. "I was worried."

She looked up at him and gave him another sweet smile. "I'll try to be more careful."

He kissed her then with all his pent-up questions and love for her. She wrapped her arms around his neck, and they were transported above everything else temporarily. When he broke off the kiss they were both breathing raggedly. He swung her up into his arms but carried her to the couch instead of their bedroom. His hunger for her came second to his need to know what was going on. He sat down with her across his lap and held her captive in his embrace. This time he couldn't wait for her to come to him. He had to know. "Nicole, I know you've been lying to me about where you've been going."

She stiffened and her eyes widened, but she didn't deny

it.

"I'm not angry, Nicole, but we will sit here until you tell me what's going on. Whatever it is, we'll face it together. Just tell me."

She inhaled sharply and blinked tears back. "I'm pregnant, Stephan. We're going to have a baby."

It took a moment for her words to sink in. "Are you sure?" *Oh, my God. I'm going to be a father.*

She nodded. "The doctor confirmed it last week."

A joy like none he'd felt before surged through him. "How far along are you?"

"Ten weeks."

He kissed her forehead and hugged her to his chest. "You went to the doctor? Which doctor? How do we know he's the best? Or is she a woman? Would a female doctor be better? We want someone who knows what they're doing."

"I went to the one my doctor suggested. Everything looks fine, but I made an appointment with Abby's obstetrician for tomorrow. Just to meet him."

"Tomorrow. What time? It doesn't matter. I'll clear my day. How do you feel? Does anything hurt?" He ran his hands down her arms.

Nicole took one of his hands in hers and laughed. "I'm pregnant, not dying."

"I'll call Dominic and see what he thought of their doctor. Have you told him yet?"

Nicole shook her head. "No, I thought we'd do it together."

Stephan kissed her on the lips briefly. "Good thinking.

What are we going to do about a room for the baby? We should make it in the one right off ours. Do you want a nanny? I know my family says they aren't important, but in the beginning you might want some extra help." He put his hand on her stomach. "Can I get you anything? Are you hungry? Do you feel sick?"

Nicole took his face between her hands. "I'm fine, Stephan. Take a deep breath. I feel fine."

"Do you know if it's a boy or girl yet?"

"It's only about this big," Nicole said and demonstrated an approximate size with her fingers.

"Right. How soon can we know and do you want to? Some people don't. I'd want to, but I can wait if it's important to you." Nicole kissed him then with such love that all coherent thought left him. He kissed her back, losing himself in the passion he never took for granted. When she ended the kiss, he couldn't stop smiling. "What was that for?"

"I love you."

He hugged her to him. "I love you, too. A baby. We're having a baby, Nicole."

Nicole returned his smile.

"My parents will lose their minds when we tell them. They love children in general, but their first grandchild? You don't even want to know what Christmas will be like this year. It doesn't matter that our little one isn't here yet; my parents will be flying relatives over from Italy just to congratulate us. Hold on to your socks, Nicole. If you thought last Christmas was wild, wait until you see one where my parents have a grandchild to celebrate."

Nicole's smile wavered, then returned. "Sounds wonderful. Hey, Abby asked us over for dinner tomorrow night. Will you be home in time to go? I'd like Dominic to hear the news from us."

Stephan looked into his wife's guarded eyes for a long moment. She was happy about the baby, he'd bet his life on it, but something was troubling her. "What's wrong, Nicole?"

She shook her head, but her smile didn't reach her eyes. "Nothing. I'm just tired, I guess."

That made sense. Coming from such a large family, Stephan had plenty of experience with pregnant women. A child in his family was a gift from above, and he'd been brought up to respect the experience of bringing one into the world. He picked Nicole up and carried her to their bedroom, placing her gently down across the bed. "I know what you want."

The warmth in her eyes lit a fire in him, but it could wait. Nicole was precious to him, and he would take his time showing her that. He slid off her shoes, sat beside her, and took one of her feet into his hands. He worked the tension out of one before reaching for her other.

Nicole burst into tears and he froze. "What's wrong?"

"You're so good to me," she said through her tears.

He crawled up onto the bed beside her and pulled her into his arms. "Don't cry, Nicole. You deserve it. You're going to be a wonderful mother." She sobbed softly against him and the sound broke his heart.

Oh boy, this is going to be a long pregnancy.

Chapter Three

ABBY CHECKED THE details of the dinner with their cook. She often made the meals for their family, but this was different. She had a feeling Nicole would need her at the table instead of running back and forth to the kitchen.

Due to the topic Nicole wanted to discuss, Abby had offered to send Judy off for a play date with her cousins, but Nicole had refused to hear it. When Judy had heard Nicole and Stephan were coming for dinner, she'd begun rushing around in excitement. If there was one thing Judy loved, it was playing hostess. She'd finished her homework early, changed into a pretty dress, and was currently helping set the table. The house staff had been with them long enough to know Abby tried to run their home as close to normal as possible, despite their level of wealth. Judy had been born into a very privileged lifestyle, but she still had chores. It was important to Abby that she appreciated what she had and how hard everyone worked to make it possible.

"Mom, Miss Jan said we're not having dessert because it's a school night."

"That's right, Judy."

"But we're having company, and they'll want dessert. Isn't it cruel if we deny them what would make them happy?"

Oh boy. Such logic might work on her father, but Abby was a harder sell. "It's Nicole and Stephan: family, not company. They'll be fine."

Judy put her hands on her hips. "They won't be happy."

Abby stopped and looked at her daughter. "Really? Why do you say that?"

Judy implored her with pleading eyes. "How could they be when I'll be sad?"

Abby ruffled her daughter's hair. "You won't be sad. You'll be on your best behavior. Are we clear?"

"Yes, Mom." Judy went back to setting the table. "I bet Auntie Lil lets her kids have dessert every night."

"I bet she doesn't."

"There is a boy at school who only eats dessert. That's it. Just cake, ice cream, candy. Whatever he wants. His parents don't care."

"Really?"

Judy's voice rose as she warmed to her tale. "Yes, in fact his doctor told him there are vitamins in ice cream so he has to eat as much of it as he can. Every day."

Abby hid her smile. "Is that true?"

Judy glanced at her mother then away. "It could be true."

Abby sighed. "How about this? What if we ask Miss Jan if she'll whip up a healthy dessert? Some frozen yogurt with berries? How does that sound?"

Judy ran over and hugged Abby's waist. "You are the best mom in the whole world."

Abby hugged her daughter. She knew from raising her sister, Lil, not every battle was worth fighting. A person could win every argument and still lose in the end. "If we ask Miss Jan really nicely I bet she'll let you help."

Judy spun with joy at the idea. "I want to be a chef like Uncle Richard. He says bad words when he cooks, and no one tells him not to. When I'm a chef I'm going to say bad words all the time, and people won't care because they'll want my food."

Not sure she wanted to hear the answer, Abby guided her daughter toward the kitchen and asked, "Do I want to know what words you're learning from Uncle Richard?"

Judy covered her mouth and giggled. "He says stupid. He says it in French, but I can understand him. He says stuuuuuupeeeed. See? I speak French."

Abby laughed out loud. "Some words are universal."

"What does universal mean?" Judy asked, but didn't wait for her mother's answer because they had reached the kitchen. "Miss Jan, Mom says we can make dessert, and I can help if you'll let me. Please. Please. Please let me."

The cook smiled and gave the stool beside her a pat. Abby had been thrilled when the woman had applied for the job. She had owned her own restaurant but left it after her husband passed. She'd said she was looking for a quieter life and that's the type of home Abby had cultivated. Miss Jan was the perfect addition. She could pull off a last-minute dinner party or serve up cereal with a smile. She also adored

Judy. That alone cemented her place in the house. "My little chef, what do you want to make?"

Judy sat straight up on the stool. "She called me a chef! That means I can say—" She stopped abruptly and looked around. "Mom, do you think Santa Claus is watching right now, or do you think he's busy wrapping presents?"

With a straight face, Abby answered, "Oh, he's watching."

Judy glanced around the room. "Does he speak French?"

Abby gave her daughter a kiss on the head. "Behave for Miss Jan. Nicole and Stephan will be here any minute. Do you mind if I run up to change?"

Miss Jan shook her head and waved her away. "We're all set. You go, Mrs. Corisi."

A few moments later Abby was reaching behind to zip the back of the simple dress she'd chosen when two strong hands finished the job. She smiled when that action was followed by a kiss to her neck.

"What time did you say Nicole and Stephan were coming over?"

Abby turned and wrapped her arms around Dominic's neck. "They'll be here any minute."

He kissed her warmly and smiled against her lips. "Damn."

Abby tipped her head back while moving her hips against his growing excitement. "You'll live."

He growled and kissed the side of her neck again up to her ear. "You never used to care if we were late to dinner."

Abby laughed. "That was before we had a child who is

not afraid to come looking for us." She pushed his roving hands away. "Now stop before I forget why this is a bad idea."

He raised his head and gave her a light tap on her tush. "Not a bad idea, just a poorly timed one. We'll continue this later."

Abby gave herself a final check in the mirror, stepped into her shoes, then took a moment to appreciate the handsome profile of her husband. "Did you have a good day?"

He smiled. "Every day that ends by coming home to you is a good one."

Abby bit her bottom lip. Dominic wasn't a man who said anything he didn't mean so when he said things like that Abby's heart still did somersault. *Tonight,* she told herself. *We can wait until tonight.*

She gave herself an inner shake. She hadn't said anything to Dominic about why Nicole was coming over because she hadn't felt it was her place, but she was beginning to wonder if she should lay a foundation for the conversation that was about to happen.

They walked out of the bedroom and down the hallway. "Dom, I've been thinking . . ."

"Yes?"

"You know how we get together every year with Lil and Jake and have a small celebration?" Dominic stopped and looked down at his wife without saying anything, so she continued. "Have you ever thought of doing that with Nicole and Stephan?"

"No."

The firmness of his answer took Abby by surprise. "It might be nice. I know we see your sister at the Andrades' for the holidays, but we could exchange presents in a smaller setting, too."

"No."

Abby stepped in front of her husband and searched his face. His expression was carefully blank. "Why not?"

The cool look he gave her would have intimidated most people, but Abby was secure in his love. She knew her question had made him uncomfortable. His normal response to feelings he didn't want to deal with was to slam a door between himself and them. The look he was giving her was nothing more than evidence that he was doing exactly that. "Drop it, Abby. I'm in a good mood. Let's just enjoy dinner."

Abby put a hand on his chest and felt his heart beating wildly there. "You're shutting me out. You promised you wouldn't do that. I love you, Dom. All of you. The best of you, and your dark secrets. You don't have to hide anything from me. Why don't you want to celebrate alone with your sister and Stephan? Talk to me, Dom."

A muscle in his jaw pulsed. "Am I a good husband to you?"

His question floored her. "Of course."

"And a good father to Judy?"

Abby searched his face for a hint that he was anything but serious. "Absolutely."

"Then respect my wishes on this. There is a rage within

me, Abby, that I keep contained so well I almost forget it's there. When we're alone, my sister digs at old wounds until I can feel the rage bubbling within me. Christmas alone with her would be hell for me. I don't want that anger in our marriage. I don't want it around Judy."

Abby stepped forward and wrapped her arms around her husband's tense body. "I understand, Dom, and it's okay."

He hugged her to him and expelled a long breath. "I love my sister."

"I know you do." Abby rested her cheek on his chest.

Suddenly dinner felt more like an ambush than the gentle prodding Abby had imagined it would be. The doorbell downstairs rang and Judy's voice called out, "They're here. Mom. Dad. Auntie Nicole and Uncle Stephan are here."

Abby held her husband tight for a moment longer and sent out a request. *Okay, Santa Claus, forget about the calorie-free eggnog I asked you to invent. That was a joke. This is serious. This year, could you bring some healing to the man I love? There has to be something that could help him let go of the past. He's a good man. His anger doesn't rule him anymore. He just needs to see that.*

DOMINIC MET HIS sister's eyes across the dinner table and felt a twinge of remorse about what he'd said to Abby earlier. Nicole had always been, and would likely always be, a fragile soul. She would never deliberately hurt anyone or knowingly cause trouble. Their problem lay in the difference in how they dealt with their demons.

As if she could read his mind, Abby took his hand in hers

and gave him a supportive smile. Hers was a gentle strength that never ceased to amaze him. She stood her ground when it was important and fought for not only herself but also everyone she loved. He was a better man because she was at his side. He would do anything for her, anything within his power anyway.

Only someone who had been held down and beaten, lived in helpless fear watching others receive the same, and vowed to never feel that way again would understand why Dominic refused to revisit that time in his life. He'd protected Nicole when he could, but he hadn't been able to protect their mother. And after their mother had left, he'd failed Nicole by leaving her with a man who had nothing but hate in his heart.

What was there to look back for? He couldn't change any of it. Remembering any part of that time only served to remind him that he'd been no better than his father. In the end, he had failed his family just as miserably.

Abby gave his hand a squeeze. "Judy, why don't you tell Auntie Nicole what you want for Christmas?"

Nicole smiled at her young niece in encouragement. "Can I guess?"

Judy clapped her hands together. "Yes. Guess. Guess."

Nicole tapped one of her manicured nails on her chin. "Is it alive?"

Judy shook her head, a move that sent her curls swaying wildly back and forth. "No. Guess again."

"Is it smaller than this table?"

Judy nodded. "Way smaller."

"A doll?"

"Nope."

"A teddy bear?"

"Not even close."

Nicole looked to her husband for help. "What do you think, Stephan? What would Judy not have a million of already?"

Stephan sat back, folded his arms across his chest. "Her own airplane?"

Judy pushed out her bottom lip. "Dad said I'm too young for that. I have to wait until I'm *sixteen*." She stressed the last word as if it were an eternity away.

Abby shook her head and laughed. "You're not getting your own plane. Not now. Not when you're sixteen."

Judy looked to her father. "But Dad said . . ."

Dominic shrugged and conceded the point to his wife. "If your mother says no, it's no."

Judy made a face. "I guess I can share yours."

Abby rolled her eyes. "The horror."

Stephan laughed. "She's going to be a handful as she gets older."

Nicole leaned toward Judy and whispered, "Ask Stephan what his cousin Maddy got when she was sixteen."

Judy bounced in her seat. "Was it a plane? Did Auntie Maddy get her own plane?"

Abby waved a hand in the air. "Don't say it, Stephan, unless you want to wear the next course."

Stephan made a motion of zipping his lips and throwing away the key.

Judy shrugged. "I'll ask Auntie Maddy. She's not a good secret keeper."

The fact that Judy already knew that about Maddy had everyone laughing. Even Dominic found himself smiling at the idea that Judy already had Maddy's number.

In the quiet that followed the laughter, Nicole put her hand on her husband's and said, "Stephan and I have news we want to share. We're having a baby."

Judy's eyes rounded. "Right now? Tonight?"

Nicole put a hand on Judy's shoulder. "No, honey, in about six months."

Dominic looked from Nicole's face to her husband's and back then nodded in approval. Stephan had proven himself so far as being good to Nicole and looked excited about the news. "Congratulations." He walked over to hug his sister then shook Stephan's hand. "I'm really happy for you both."

Abby hugged both Nicole and Stephan. "I'm so excited for you."

Judy crawled onto Nicole's lap. "Where is it?"

"The baby?" Nicole asked.

"Yes."

Nicole rested a hand on her stomach. "It's in here."

"Why don't you have a big belly?" Judy asked.

"I will," Nicole said with a laugh. "It's early yet. The baby has to grow."

Judy put her hand on Nicole's stomach. "There's a baby in there? Right now? How does it get in there?"

Dominic held back a laugh and Stephan coughed.

Abby said, "We'll talk about all that later, Judy. Just say

congratulations for now."

Judy snuggled against Nicole. "Congratulations. You're going to be a mom. I hope you get someone like me. I make my parents happy."

"Yes, you do," Dominic said and earned a huge smile from his wife.

Nicole hugged her closer and over her head said, "When I found out I was pregnant, I started thinking about Christmas—"

Abby knocked a glass of water over. "Oh, my God, look at that, I'm so clumsy sometimes."

Everyone handed her their napkins and Dominic called for the housekeeper who came quickly and cleaned up the mess. When everything was settled again, Nicole said, "As I was saying, I've been thinking that this year—"

Abby stood. "Nicole. Can I talk to you in the kitchen for a moment?"

Stephan turned his wife's hand over in his and gave her a long look. "I have an idea. The holidays are crazy around here. What do you think if this year we do something small, just the four of us?" He winked at Judy. "Five of us. We could fly over to Isola Santos the week before Christmas and celebrate there before we come back and celebrate here. We never do anything with just us. It might be nice."

Nicole gave her husband a teary smile. "Would you really be okay with that? I've been trying to find a way to ask you if we could do that, but I was afraid you'd think I didn't enjoy Christmas with your family. I do. I just want one Christmas with mine."

"No," Dominic said. He met Abby's guilty gaze and realized she'd known what Nicole wanted to ask. Their conversation from earlier suddenly made sense. Anger began to spread inside him, but he clenched his teeth and kept his thoughts to himself.

Nicole gasped at the abruptness of his tone, and Stephan put his arm protectively around her.

Abby walked over to where Judy was still sitting on Nicole. "Judy, why don't we go see if Miss Jan has the dessert ready?"

Judy looked around at the suddenly tense-looking adults and said, "Mommy, what happened?"

"Nothing, Baby. Let's go."

"But—"

Abby gave her daughter a look that ended whatever Judy had been about to ask. Abby paused in front of Dominic. "I'll be one minute."

As soon as she'd cleared the kitchen door, Stephan stood and said, "What the hell is your problem tonight, Dominic?"

Nicole put a hand on his arm. Her eyes were shining with tears. "Don't, Stephan. I knew he wouldn't want to. I shouldn't have asked."

Normally Dominic would have said something cutting back to Stephan, but he was protecting Nicole and Dominic couldn't hate him for that. The last thing Dominic wanted to do was hurt his sister, but the scene unraveling over dinner was exactly why a Corisi Christmas shouldn't happen.

Stephan approached Dominic, his voice rising with anger as he did. He stopped within inches of Dominic. "Pick a side, Dominic. Either you're a loving brother or an asshole who I won't let anywhere near my wife."

This is the man my sister loves. He's the father of the child within her. "Don't come between my family and me, Stephan. It's a dangerous place."

Stephan didn't back down. He snarled, "I'd take your own advice, Dominic. Nicole and our baby, that's my family. You hurt them, and you'll spend the rest of your life regretting you did."

Abby returned and stepped between them, putting a hand up. "No one is hurting anyone. Both of you take a deep breath."

Neither man did. They both remained postured for what was moving toward a physical altercation. Between gritted teeth, Dominic said, "I would never do anything to hurt my sister."

Stephan fired back, "What do you think you just did?"

"Please stop," Nicole said, looking back and forth between them with tears running down her face.

Abby took the two men each by one arm and turned them toward Nicole. "Do either of you think you're helping Nicole feel better, or are you both so wrapped up in yourself that you can't see you're upsetting her?"

Dominic saw real distress in his sister's face and was overcome with anger at himself. He hated that he couldn't be the brother she needed, not when they were younger and not now. Stephan had every right to call him every name in the book. This was what he'd wanted to avoid. He met Abby's eyes briefly then strode out of the room.

Chapter Four

NICOLE WAS SHAKING. Stephan was talking to her, but he sounded far away. In her mind she was reliving what Dominic had said and fighting back the fear that she could lose her brother again.

Abby looked at Stephan. "We can't work this out for them, Stephan. No matter how much we want to." She took one of Nicole's hands in hers. "Nicole, Dominic loves you. He's not angry with you, he's angry with himself. As hard as it is to imagine, inside that man is a young boy who wanted to save you and your mother from your father and failed. That's what he hates. That's why he's afraid to look back. You're about to become a mother. Not everything your child says to you will be kind, but you have to be strong enough to love them through that. Learn that skill here. Dominic needs you right now. He can't ask you to be there for him. He doesn't know how. He's hurting as much as you are. Go in there and give him a hug. I promise you it's what you both need."

Stephan opened his mouth but held his thought to himself when Abby raised a hand and said, "Trust me on this one. Please."

Nicole clasped her hands in front of her. "He won't want to talk to me."

Abby looked at the door Dominic had walked out of. "So don't say anything. Just give him a hug."

Nicole met her husband's eyes. He was angry. He was worried. He wanted to tell her not to go, but he also knew how important her brother was to her. In that moment Nicole saw the strength of Stephan's love. Words were easy to say, but he put his pride *and* his anger aside for her.

Nicole squared her shoulders and nodded. She had always relied on Dominic to be the strong one. Maybe change would only come when their roles flipped. She walked out the door of the dining room and saw Dominic standing near his desk in his office. Without saying a word, Nicole walked to him and wrapped her arms around him. His arms instantly came up to embrace her, and he hugged her tightly.

In the past Nicole would have said something. She would have tried to fix what was broken between them, but she heeded Abby's advice. She hugged him back and let her questions and insecurities fall away. She wasn't turning to him for help or feeling scared he would leave her. This time, if only for a moment, she was the strong one.

He dropped his arms and stepped back. "I'm sorry, Nicole. I know what you want, but—"

Nicole saw her brother through Abby's eyes, and it was a revelation. Dominic wasn't saying no because he didn't want to be with her. He was saying no because he was afraid. Fear was something she understood far too well. She touched his arm gently. "I get it now. It's okay."

"No. Stephan was right. I didn't have to say no the way I did. I don't want you to think—"

"I know you love me, Dom. I love you. That's all that matters."

Dominic looked away as he spoke. "I hate him, and I hate who I am because of him."

Nicole didn't have to ask who he was talking about. Dominic only hated one man—their father. Nicole put her arms around her brother again. Abby's insight into Dominic helped shape what Nicole said next. "We are more than what he did to us, Dom. You are more than whatever you regret doing. You have a temper. I'm a nervous wreck. So what? You have an amazing wife and a beautiful daughter. I have a man I love so much it hurts and a child on the way. Instead of looking back at everything we did wrong, can we remember some of what we did right? This year, I'm going to give you something that is technically already yours and you are going to love it. And I want you to give me something that is already mine. That's it. That's all I want for Christmas. Can you do that?"

Dominic relaxed. "Yes, I can."

Nicole took her brother by the arm and together they walked back into the dining room. Abby and Stephan were both carefully quiet.

Judy rushed back into the room. "Mom, Miss Jan said the yogurt isn't ready. Can we have cake instead?"

"Sure," Abby said without taking her eyes off Dominic.

Judy's jaw dropped open. "Yes?" She looked to her father

for confirmation. "Really?"

"Whatever you want, Judy, just go get it," Abby said.

Judy hesitated. "It's a school night. Are you sure you want me to have all that sugar?"

Abby turned to look at her daughter. "What did you say?"

Judy's eyes rounded innocently. "Nothing. Dad, you heard her, she said yes."

Dominic stared at Judy for a moment, then a smile spread across his face. "She did. Why don't you have Miss Jan bring out cake for everyone?" He walked over and slid an arm around Abby's waist. "Thank you."

Nicole watched her brother and his wife exchange a few more words quietly, and it warmed her heart. Stephan came up behind Nicole and wrapped his arms around her. "Did you work things out?"

Nicole nodded. "We did."

"Are we getting together for Christmas?"

Nicole leaned back against Stephan, loving how safe he made her feel. "I don't know, but I'm not worried about it anymore. Abby was right; he needed a hug."

Stephan made a sound in his throat but didn't disagree. "I'm sorry I flew at him like that. I don't know what came over me."

Nicole hugged his arms closer around her. In a voice low enough so Abby and Dominic couldn't hear, Nicole said, "Don't knock down Dominic's house on Isola Santos. I want to give it to him for Christmas."

"How about we demolish it, but build him a new one?

It's an eyesore."

In the past, Nicole would have relented, worried if she said what she really wanted, Stephan would be angry. Embracing her faults, though, was helping her overcome them. "Dominic built that house, and it's beautiful to him. This will show him we accept him the way he is."

"We couldn't just get a card that says that?" Stephan joked.

Nicole elbowed him.

"Okay. Okay. I'll call off the demolition. But when you're standing on your beautiful Italian balcony and all you can see is a reflection of yourself in the enormous glass windows of his home, it's on you."

Nicole turned her head to kiss Stephan's cheek. "I love you."

He turned his head so their lips met briefly. "I love you, too. Any chance you want to be the one to explain this to Gio?"

LATER THAT NIGHT Dominic and Abby stood in the doorway of Judy's bedroom, watching her sleep. Dominic tucked his wife into his side and said, "I didn't think she'd ever fall asleep."

"That's what we get for giving her cake so late in the day."

Giving in to the temptation to tease her, Dominic said, "Who said yes?"

Abby swatted his chest. "I was distracted by all the testosterone. I thought you and Stephan were going to wrestle each other to the floor."

"I would have won," Dominic said, and earned himself another swat. He didn't care. He grabbed Abby's hand, brought it to his mouth and kissed it. "Nicole wants me to give her something that's already hers. We used to do that when we were kids."

"I know. She told me the story."

"I was an ass tonight. I should have agreed to celebrate Christmas with them."

"You weren't ready to. I think Nicole understands that now."

"How did I end up with such a wise wife?"

Abby shot him a cheeky smile. "You were that good in bed."

His eyebrows shot up in pleased surprise. "I figured as much."

"So, what are you going to give Nicole?"

"I don't know."

Abby chewed her bottom lip for a moment in an uncharacteristic moment of uncertainty. "I have an idea, but I don't know if it's a good one."

Dominic studied her face for a long moment. He knew that expression. Whatever she was about to say was something she'd been thinking about for a while. "Just say it."

"Do you remember that box Nicole found in your father's things? She wouldn't open it because she was too afraid of what would be inside it. You wouldn't open it for the same reason—"

"I'm not—"

"I know. But the box has been in the attic for years now. Stephan said she still visits your father's grave."

"I didn't know Nicole—"

"She does. She always has. She's just too afraid to tell you. I know you say you hate your father, Dom, but Nicole loved him. What if there is something in that box she would want?"

Dominic tensed at the mere thought of looking at something his father had owned. "There is nothing in there I want to see."

"I peeked inside, Dom. There is an envelope addressed to both you and Nicole."

He didn't blame her for being curious because she'd never met the piece of work that was his father. "If I know him it's some sick document claiming that Nicole and I aren't even . . ."

"Even what?"

"My father was a bastard. He'd do or say anything to hurt us, even from the grave."

Abby hugged him. "He can't hurt you anymore, no matter what is in that envelope. You need to prove that to yourself. Open the box. Tear open that envelope. Don't let your father define you."

Dominic didn't promise anything, but Abby's suggestion came back to him several times the next day. Every time he thought about his sister, he wondered what he could possibly give her for Christmas, and then an image of the box would fill his head.

He waited until both Abby and Judy were sleeping and

retrieved the box from the attic. He took it to his office and set it on his desk.

Abby was right. His father couldn't hurt him or his family anymore. No matter what was in the box, it wouldn't change anything. He removed the cover and picked up the envelope addressed to Nicole and him. Instead of opening it, he walked to the fireplace and held it above the flames. *I don't care about you or whatever you wanted me to know.*

The paper on the envelope darkened, but Dominic pulled it back from the flames before it caught fire. He tore it open. Inside was a handwritten letter from his father.

Dominic,

Thomas Brogos just left with my new will. The doctors say I don't have much time left and something about facing death has made me rethink a few things.

My father was a vicious drunk. I'm not saying that as an excuse, it's merely a fact. There is a rage inside of me I've never successfully contained. I fear I've passed that rage down to you.

I would apologize, but there was never anything my father could have said that would have made me hate him less. I hated who he was and the man I became because of him.

Dominic dropped the letter to the desk as if stung by it. He'd spent most of his life afraid he would become his father and there, in black and white, were his own words written by his father. With a shaking hand, Dominic picked the letter back up and continued to read it.

I thought I had it all, but in the end I drove my wife away, made my son an enemy, and watched my daughter cry tears for a father who had done nothing to earn her love.

Don't make the same mistakes I did. Don't bequeath your rage to your children. Let it die with me.

I can't go back and undo anything I've done. I can't be the father you should have had, but I can do one thing right. You and your sister would have been closer if it weren't for me. I'm leaving the company to her under the stipulation that you run it for a year. Use that year wisely. Find your way back to being a family.

She's angry with you, Dominic, but you were not the one who failed her. That was me. Forgive her, no matter what she says to you. Forgive yourself, no matter how many times you look in the mirror and see me.

Nicole,

Don't hate your brother for what I did to both of you. Don't hate your mother for leaving. The weight of all of that rests on my shoulders alone.

You stayed by me when everyone else left. I know you think I didn't care about you, but I had to pull away, otherwise I would have hurt you, too.

Take this time with your brother to get to know each other again. Forgive him. There is darkness in his heart, but I put it there.

You're still here with me, Nicole. I could tell you this in person instead of writing it down, but there is too much I'd have to say. I'm sorry I am taking the easy way out.

I loved you both. My greatest regret is that I will die without either of you knowing it or being better because of it.

Your father

Dominic tucked the letter into the inside breast pocket of his suit jacket and replaced the cover to the box. His mind was racing as he replayed the letter over and over again in his head.

His father had given in to the rage within him, and it had destroyed not only him, but his family as well. Dominic would never lay a hand on his wife or his child, but he was at times ruled by the anger within him.

He stood in his office with his hands clenched. A confusing mix of emotions swirled within him. He didn't want to pity his father. He wanted to hate him, but hadn't it been hate that had made his father into who he was?

A small hand closed around Dominic's. He looked down to see Judy had taken his hand in hers. "Dad, are you okay?"

He forced a smile and picked her up. "What are you doing up?"

"I had a nightmare."

"Me, too," Dominic said to himself.

"I dreamed everyone was fighting."

That sounds about right, Dominic thought but didn't say aloud.

Judy patted her father's face with her hands. "What did you dream about?"

"It doesn't matter."

"Mom says that talking about bad dreams makes them go away. You don't want to have the dream again, do you? You'd better tell me."

Dominic kissed his daughter's forehead. "I dreamed I did something to make Auntie Nicole sad, and I didn't know how to make it right."

Judy smiled. "That's easy, what does she want for Christmas? Give it to her now. Everyone loves presents."

Dominic thought about it and laughed at the simplicity of Judy's solution. "You're a genius, Judy."

"I know," Judy said with a huge smile. Then she frowned and asked, "What's a genius?"

Chapter Five

NICOLE LOOKED OUT the window of their private plane as it circled Isola Santos, the Andrades' private island. "You're really not going to tell me what my surprise is?"

"I'm really not," Stephan answered.

"But we had to come all the way here to get it?"

"We did."

"It's dangerous to mess with a pregnant woman's emotions. I'd rather just know what we're doing here."

Stephan gave her hand a squeeze. "You've made it this far. I can't tell you now." He leaned over and gave her a kiss. "Trust me."

"I do," Nicole answered without hesitation. In the past week, Stephan had proven to her again and again that she was a priority to him. He'd attended doctor appointments, gone shopping for baby items with her, and hovered over her, making sure she wanted for nothing.

He'd suggested they not go to his family that Christmas, but Nicole had had a change of heart. She couldn't imagine missing an Andrade holiday. And if she and her brother could only connect at a gathering like that, then so be it. She would meet him where he needed to be.

Stephan's announcement that they needed to fly to his family's island the weekend before Christmas had come as a surprise. He wasn't saying why, but Nicole guessed it had something to do with the talk they'd had about how she wanted to start family traditions of their own. Or he simply wanted her to see their completed home on the island.

The plane landed and as they stepped out onto the runway Nicole noticed Dominic's plane on the other runway. She wrapped her coat tighter around her against the cold island wind. "Is my brother here?"

Stephan's chest puffed with pride. "He and his family flew in this morning. I hope you don't mind, but I had our home decked out for the holiday. Next year we can come early and decorate."

Nicole's eyes filled with happy tears. "How did you get him to come?"

Stephan guided Nicole up the steps of their new home. "He called me. He said he had a present for you. I told him you had something for him, but he'd have to fly here to get it."

Just outside their new front door Nicole threw her arms around Stephan's neck. "Every time I think I couldn't love you more, you find a way to make me fall in love with you all over again." She kissed him deeply. In that moment everything else fell away and it was just Nicole and the man she loved. The passion she'd always felt for him was there, pulsing within her, but years together had given it a depth she'd never imagined. She didn't just want him; she needed him. His touch, his body thrusting into hers, was as vital to her as the air she was raggedly taking in. She writhed against him, digging her hands into his hair. "Do you think we have time before they come over?"

Stephan took out his phone and sent a quick text. "We do now." He opened the door, swung her up into his arms, and carried her over the threshold.

Nicole kissed his neck and laughed as he took the steps two at a time. "What did you say?"

He lowered her to her feet just inside a large bedroom. "I told them we'd see them at six."

Nicole buried her face in his shoulder. "Do you think they know?"

Stephan took a clip out of the back of Nicole's hair and released it. "Do you care?"

She shook her head. "My goal for the new year is to be more honest about what I want."

A lusty smile spread across her husband's face. "I like that."

Nicole would describe their sex life as healthy and heated, but she didn't often take the lead in the bedroom. She enthusiastically went where he took her, but she had fantasies she'd never dared voice. "Do you? What else do you like?"

His eyes burned with passion for her. "I love the feel of your lips around my cock. I love burying myself deeply inside you as you call out my name."

Nicole ran a hand down Stephan's chest and cupped his erection. She said something she'd never dared to before. "You'll have to earn those pleasures this time."

His face flushed with excitement. "I'm yours to command."

Nicole hesitated, but desire flamed through her and made her bold. "Strip me."

He fell easily into the game. "With pleasure." After he removed an article of clothing he worshiped the exposed area with his mouth and hands before moving on to remove another piece.

"Kneel and don't stop licking until I come."

Fully dressed, he sank to his knees before her and lifted one leg, placing it over his shoulder. "You're so fucking hot when you talk like that, Nicole."

Nicole held on to a bedpost to steady herself and closed her eyes. "Stop talking and start licking. I want to feel you pumping a finger in and out of me."

Stephan was a gifted lover, but he was particularly skilled in the oral sex department. He licked around her clit, teased her until she was digging a hand into his shoulder, and took her gently between his teeth.

She was wet and ready for his finger when he slid it inside her and started to do his magical circular motions that always drove her crazy. "Oh, God, yes."

His tongue began to flick back and forth over her clit, slowly at first, then faster and faster. She called out with pleasure when she finally came, and he picked her up and tossed her down on the bed.

"What else do you want?" he asked in a hungry, husky tone as he stripped off his own clothing. "Tell me."

"I want to be this happy for the rest of my life," she said, loving each part of him he uncovered.

"I can do that." He crawled onto the bed and positioned himself above her, then rolled until she was sprawled on top. "But I was hoping for something a little more specific."

She smiled down at him. She wasn't assertive by nature, but his love was her safety net. "Then slide yourself inside me and quit your chatting."

He did, and together they went to a place they'd gone many times before, but this time was more playful than it had been in a while. When she lay in his arms afterward, she thought about something his mother had once told her about how to make a marriage work. "Honesty. Respect. Forgiveness. And a little red bikini."

The longer she was married, the more wisdom Nicole found in those words. The bikini symbolized keeping the passion fresh and exciting. Naked in her husband's arms, Nicole vowed to do just that. She leaned forward and kissed him, thrusting her tongue deep into his mouth and teasing his into hers. "Now, you tell me what you want."

Stephan groaned and checked the clock on the bedside table. "We don't have time."

Nicole leaned off the bed, found his phone and sent a text. "We do now," she said cheekily.

"I told him I'm getting an early Christmas present."

Stephan grabbed the phone, looked at it, and tossed it onto the floor. "You sent it from my phone? Your brother will kill me, but I'll worry about that later. Come here, wife."

Nicole laughed, a little embarrassed. "Sorry. Do you want me to send another text explaining it?"

"No," he growled against her neck. "I want you to make it up to me."

"I can do that, but you'll have to be a little more specific."

ABBY CHECKED THE time on her phone. "It's seven thirty. Do you think it's safe to head over there now?"

Dominic stood by the tall glass-paned wall and glared at the other house. "For them or for us?"

Abby tucked herself beneath her husband's arm. "Have a sense of humor, it's almost Christmas." When Dominic didn't respond, Abby chided, "They're married, and your sister is pregnant. How do you think that happened?"

He made a face. "It's my little sister."

"Who is a grown woman with a husband she loves. Be happy for her."

Dominic sighed. "You're right." He glanced over his shoulder. "Where's Judy?"

"She's pretending not to be peeking at the pile of gifts we left in the hall. It was a good idea to bring them. I know we'll see my family and the Andrades for Christmas, but it helps Judy understand what this is about, too. It's a lot of celebrating for one holiday."

"We have a big family."

Abby smiled and rested her head on Dominic's shoulder. "We do. We certainly do." Abby sent a text to Stephan. "Get dressed we're coming over." If it weren't for Judy, Abby would have let the lovebirds have their time together, but they'd told Judy their plans for the evening, and she wasn't about to try to explain to her why they couldn't go over to see her aunt and uncle.

Judy came rushing in. "Is it time yet? Can we go?"

Abby laughed. "Patience, Judy. Yes, we can head over."

"Do I get to open all of my presents now?"

"What do you think, Dom?" Abby asked.

"My mother comes tomorrow morning, and she'll bring presents. Your sister will have something when we go there. The Andrades will have more. I say yes."

"Don't forget Santa," Judy added.

"And Santa," Dominic agreed.

Like a puppy excited to go outside, Judy ran circles around them as they gathered up their coats and packages. "This is going to be awesome."

With each of them carrying several packages, Dominic, Abby, and Judy crossed the lawn between the home Dominic had built years before and the new home Stephan had built to replace it. When Nicole opened the door her face was beautifully flushed, and she was smiling.

"Sorry about the delay," Nicole said, trying to sound contrite, but her smile didn't waver.

Dominic gave Stephan a narrow-eyed look that his brother-in-law merely shrugged off. "Time just got away from us," Stephan said.

Dominic handed Stephan some packages with more force than the action called for. "Mind holding these for me?"

"Not at all," Stephan answered without looking the least bit upset.

They walked together into a room displaying an elegantly decorated Christmas tree and a crackling fire in the fireplace. Judy handed her boxes to Nicole and sprinted over to the tree. "There's one for me and there's one for you, Dad." She went back to hold her mother's hand. "Don't worry, Mom, I have one for you."

Abby gave her daughter a quick hug. "I have everything I need, but thank you."

Nicole deposited the boxes Judy had given her beside the tree and blushed. "Abby, the gift for Dominic is really for both of you."

Abby waved a hand and took a seat. "With all of you here, I have everything I need. When your little one arrives you'll see that the best gifts are the ones you watch your child open."

Dominic sat beside Abby. "I agree."

Judy climbed onto Dominic's lap. "Me, too."

Everyone laughed at that.

Nicole retrieved an envelope from beneath the tree and handed it to her brother. "This is from Stephan and me. It's something that was yours, and we want you to have it again."

Dominic opened the envelope and read the paper inside twice before handing it to Abby. It was the deed to the house he'd built on the island. A huge smile spread across his face. "Abby, I told you it was too beautiful to knock down. I'm glad someone else agreed with me."

Stephan looked as if he were trying not to laugh. "That's what it was, the beauty of it."

Nicole chuckled and gave Stephan a nudge. "This is a

family island and you're family. Your house belongs here."

Dominic cleared his throat and pulled an envelope out of his coat pocket. "I have something for you, Nicole. I hope it makes you as happy as you've just made me."

Judy said softly, "Those gifts don't look that exciting."

Abby corrected her gently, "It's never the gift that's important, Judy; it's the love behind it that matters. Remember that."

Nicole started to cry as she read the letter, then she stood and rushed over to give Dominic a kiss on the cheek. "Thank you. This is exactly what I needed."

"Me, too. I love you, Nicole. And things are going to be better from now on. I promise."

Judy was momentarily squished between them when Nicole threw her arms around Dominic. Judy peered out at her mother from between her father and her aunt and said, "I guess grownups like mail."

Abby laughed. "I guess they do."

Nicole walked back and handed the letter to Stephan who nodded as he read it, then hugged her. He blinked several times, and his eyes shone with emotion as he said, "Thank you, Dominic."

Dominic took Abby's hand in his. "Thank you, Stephan, for being so good to my sister. We're lucky to have you in our family."

Abby gave her husband's hand a squeeze.

Judy turned to Dominic. "Now can I open one of mine? Please?"

Dominic eased her onto her feet. "Go pick one out,

Princess."

Judy placed the gifts in a row and read over each tag of the most important presents beneath the tree. "Uncle Jeremy and Auntie Jeisa. Auntie Zhang and Uncle Rachid. Auntie Alethea and Uncle Marc. Uncle Stephan and Auntie Nicole. Which one do I open first?"

"How about the one from Nicole and Stephan?" Abby suggested.

Nicole knelt beside her niece. "Open it. I hope you like it."

Abby said, "She'll like it. No matter what it is. Right, Judy? We're always grateful for anything anyone gives us."

Judy rolled her eyes and quietly said to Nicole, "She was a teacher, and she can't turn it off." Louder she said, "Yes, Mom." She ripped open the package and clapped. "It's an airplane. Does it fly?"

Nicole sat back and nodded. "It sure does."

Judy hugged Nicole. "You rock. Thanks. And it flies. That's cool." She picked up a small box. "This one is for you and Uncle Stephan. It's from me."

Nicole carried it over to Stephan. She opened it and held up the handmade frame Abby had helped Judy decorate. "It's beautiful."

Judy smiled. "You can put a picture of me holding your baby when it comes. That way you have two people you love in one picture."

Nicole wiped tears from the corners of her eyes. "What a perfect gift, Judy. Just perfect."

Judy reached for another gift. "Mom said we have to take

turns opening them, so Dad is next." She walked a large rectangular box over to her father. "Dad, this is for you and Mom. Uncle Jake helped me pick it out."

She handed it to Dominic who held it out to Abby, but Abby said, "No, you can open it."

Dominic removed the paper and the cover of the box, then one of his eyebrows rose as he studied the contents.

Judy pulled one of the garments out of the box and held it up. "They're pajamas for Christmas. Look, Dad. You get to be Santa. Mom gets to be Mrs. Claus, and I'm an elf. Isn't that awesome? Can we wear them tonight?"

Dominic looked over at Abby who smiled back at him. "Remember, it's the love behind the gift that matters."

"When do we see Jake and Lil?" Dominic asked with a growing grin.

"Thursday."

"That should be enough time for me to find the perfect presents for his children."

"Dominic . . ." Abby started to say, then gave in to the fun of the idea. "I'll help you."

Judy picked up another present and opened it. "Auntie Zhang sent me a real princess dress. She says I can look like her now." Judy spun with it. "I love it."

She looked over at her parents. "Can I open another?"

"Go ahead," Abby said, and Dominic put an arm around his wife.

She tore the wrapping off the next gift. She looked at the pictures on the box and turned it around a few times. "What is it?"

Abby went onto the floor beside her daughter. "It looks like Alethea and Marc sent you a spy kit."

"That's what we need, for her to see *more* of what's going on in the house," Dominic joked.

Judy clapped her hands together happily. "I'm going to be a spy when I grow up, just like Auntie Alethea. She's so cool."

"Not a princess like Auntie Zhang?" Nicole asked with humor.

Judy gave Nicole a look as if to say there was no comparison. "A princess wears a tiara and has to sit pretty. A spy gets to sneak around and look at everything."

Abby looked over at Dominic. "Are we letting her spend too much time with Alethea and Marc?"

Judy was already onto the next present. "Uncle Jeremy sends the best gifts. Remember last year he gave me a robot that knew my name." She ripped the present open and frowned. "It's a button." She looked at the words written on it and sounded them out. "Pr-ess h-ere. Press here." Then she did.

All the cell phones in the room buzzed and started playing one of her favorite winter Disney songs. She pressed it again and they all switched to another Disney song. "That is so cool."

"I'm going to kill him," Dominic said as he looked at his phone and couldn't figure out how to get the music to stop.

Judy brought a note over to Abby. "What does it say, Mom?"

"It says press the button again then take a picture of your

father's expression with someone's phone and send it to Uncle Jeremy."

Judy laughed and used her mother's phone to take several photos, then she swiped back and forth between the best of them. "Which one do you like best, Dad?"

"You pick one, Princess." Dominic looked at Abby and shook his head. "People used to fear me."

Judy climbed back up onto his lap. "Why would anyone be afraid of you?" She hugged him. "You're just a big, old, grumpy teddy bear."

Dominic hugged his daughter to his chest. He closed his eyes for a moment, and Abby's heart melted. Dominic had survived a hellish childhood and, unlike his father, he had not passed his rage on to his child. Watching him finally see that was the best Christmas present Abby had ever received.

Chapter Six

A WEEK LATER Nicole was holding Stephan's hand and mingling in the Andrade home in New York. She'd lost count of how many times she'd been hugged and congratulated on her pregnancy since Stephan and she had arrived. Instead of being overwhelmed as she had feared she'd feel, she basked in the warmth of their love.

Over the past week, she'd read and reread her father's letter. His final words had given her what she had needed to set herself free from her fears. He had been an extremely troubled man, but he'd loved her. And Dominic had shown his love for her by facing the past. How could she be afraid, when her life was full of so many people who cared about her?

Stephan leaned down and said, "Tell me when you get tired and we'll go."

She hugged his arm to her. "I know I said I didn't want to come this year, but I'm so glad we did. I wanted a Corisi Christmas, and I got one, but this is also my family. Thank you for understanding that this year I needed to heal one family before I could appreciate the other."

He kissed her on the temple. "My Christmas will always be wherever you are, Nicole." He looked down at her stomach. "You and our child. Without you, I wouldn't be here, either. I was lost once, and you guided me back to my family. If you ever feel afraid again, don't hide it. Reach for me because I'll always be right here, beside you."

Before Nicole had a chance to answer Stephan, his father, Victor, swung her away from him and off her feet into a hug. "Merry Christmas, Nicole."

Stephan's mother said, "Victor, put her down." She shook her head. "Stephan, ever since you told us Nicole's pregnant, your father has been as loopy as your Uncle Alessandro. He's picking out toys already."

Victor was all unapologetic smiles. "I'm going to be a grandfather. Finally. I can't tell you how happy I am."

Nicole met her brother's approving gaze from across the room, then looked back at Stephan who was beaming with pride, and his parents who were gushing with love for her and the child they would spoil rotten. Nicole linked hands with Stephan and smiled. Christmas was a time for new beginnings and for letting go of things no longer relevant. No matter what the future held for her, Nicole knew she was where she belonged. She had found her voice, and no one had walked away.

It was a Christmas she'd never forget and one she'd always be grateful for.

THE END

Want more of Dominic Corisi?

Get book one of the Barrington Billionaires: Always Mine.

Or

In the mood for a spicy holiday romance? Recipe for Love will warm your heart with the story of how Maddy met Richard.

Or

Looking for a way to get onto Santa's naughty list? My hottest Christmas romance is about Brock and Kate in the Temptation Series:

12 Days of Temptation and Be My Temptation.

Other Books by Ruth

The Legacy Collection:

****Also available in audiobook format***

Where my billionaires began.

Book 1: Maid for the Billionaire (available at all major eBook stores for FREE!)

Book 2: For Love or Legacy

Book 3: Bedding the Billionaire

Book 4: Saving the Sheikh

Book 5: Rise of the Billionaire

Book 6: Breaching the Billionaire: Alethea's Redemption

Book 7: A Corisi Christmas Novella

The Andrades

****Also available in audiobook format***

A spin off series of the Legacy Collection with cameos from characters you love from that series.

Book 1: Come Away With Me (available at all major eBook stores for FREE!)

Book 2: Home to Me

Book 3: Maximum Risk

Book 4: Somewhere Along the Way

Book 5: Loving Gigi

Recipe For Love, An Andrade Christmas Novella

The Barringtons

A new, seven book series about the Andrade's Boston cousins.

The first series in the Barrington Billionaire WORLD.

Book 1: Always Mine

Book 2: Stolen Kisses (Available for Pre-order)

Book 3: Trade It All (Coming 2016)

Book 4: Let It Burn (Coming 2016)

Book 5: More Than Love (Coming 2016)

Book 6: Forever Now (Coming 2016)

Book 7: Never Goodbye (Coming 2016)

*Look for a linked series set in the same world, written by Jeannette Winters (my sister).

You won't have to read her series to enjoy mine, but it sure will make it more fun. Characters will appear in both series.

Author Jeannette Winters

Book 1: One White Lie (Coming late 2015)

Book 2: Table for Two

Book 3: You & Me Make Three

Book 4: Virgin for the Fourth Time

Book 5: His for Five Nights

Book 6: After Six

My characters also appear in her Betting on You Series in the Billionaire's Longshot.

Book 1: The Billionaire's Secret (FREE!)

Book 2: The Billionaire's Masquerade

Book 3: The Billionaire's Longshot

Book 4: The Billionaire's Jackpot

Novella: All Bets Off

Lone Star Burn Series:

Fun, hot romances that roam from the country to the city and back.

Book 1: Taken, Not Spurred

Book 2: Tycoon Takedown

Book 3: (Coming soon)

The Temptation Series:

Guaranteed to put you on Santa's naughty list.

Twelve Days of Temptation and Be My Temptation

Two hot novellas about one sizzling couple.

Other Books:

Taken By a Trillionaire

Ruth Cardello, JS Scott, Melody Anne.

Three hot fantasies about alpha princes and the women who tame them.

About the Author

Ruth Cardello was born the youngest of 11 children in a small city in northern Rhode Island. She spent her young adult years moving as far away as she could from her large extended family. She lived in Boston, Paris, Orlando, New York—then came full circle and moved back to Rhode Island. She now happily lives one town over from the one she was born in. For her, family trumped the warmer weather and international scene.

She was an educator for 20 years, the last 11 as a kindergarten teacher. When her school district began cutting jobs, Ruth turned a serious eye toward her second love– writing and has never been happier. When she's not writing, you can find her chasing her children around her small farm, riding her horses, or connecting with her readers online.

Contact Ruth:

Website: RuthCardello.com

Email: Minouri@aol.com

FaceBook: Author Ruth Cardello

Twitter: @RuthieCardello

Sign up for Ruth's Mailing List

One random newsletter subscriber will be chosen every month in 2015. The chosen subscriber will receive a $100 eGift Card! Sign up today at ruthcardello.com!

Made in the USA
San Bernardino, CA
19 May 2020